# The Adirondack Kids® #13

## The Carousel Case, The Bicycle Race & The Blackfly Bad Guy

By Justin & Gary VanRiper
Illustrations by Carol VanRiper

Adirondack Kids Press, Ltd.
Camden, New York

The Adirondack Kids® #13
The Carousel Case, The Bicycle Race &
The Blackfly Bad Guy

Justin & Gary VanRiper


First Paperback Edition, May 2013

Cover illustration by Susan Loeffler
Illustrated by Carol McCurn VanRiper



Published by
Adirondack Kids Press, Ltd.
39 Second Street
Camden, New York 13316
www.adirondackkids.com

Printed in the United States of America
by Patterson Printing, Michigan

Paper — $9.95 — ISBN 978-0-9826250-3-3

Dedication

To Joanna VanRiper

on our first
wedding anniversary

— Justin

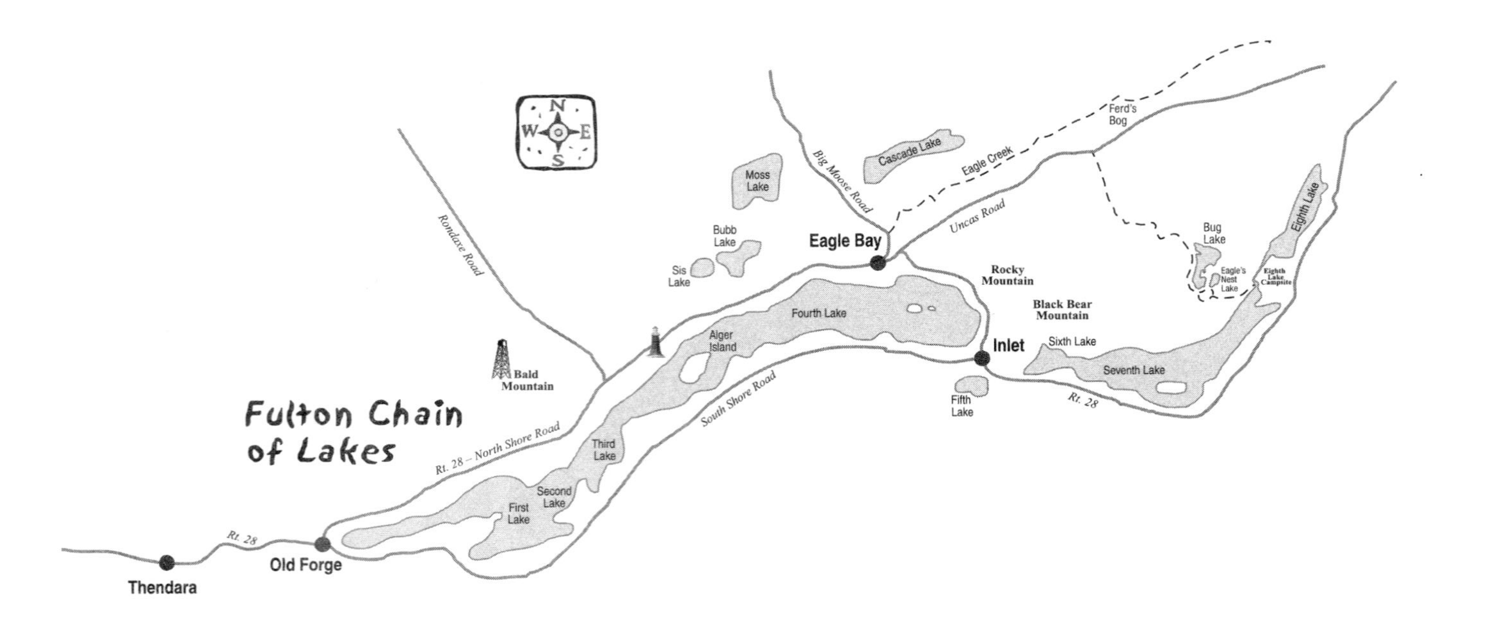
Fulton Chain of Lakes
N
W
E
S
Rondaxe Road
Bald Mountain
Rt. 28 – North Shore Road
Moss Lake
Bubb Lake
Sis Lake
Big Moose Road
Cascade Lake
Eagle Creek
Ferd's Bog
Uncas Road
Eagle Bay
Rocky Mountain
Black Bear Mountain
Bug Lake
Eagle's Nest Lake
Eighth Lake Campsite
Eighth Lake
Fourth Lake
Alger Island
Third Lake
Second Lake
First Lake
South Shore Road
Inlet
Fifth Lake
Sixth Lake
Seventh Lake
Rt. 28
Rt. 28
Old Forge
Thendara

# Contents


1 – What's All the BUZZ? ..................1
2 – Bye-Bye Blackfly ..................4
3 – The Bug Lake Bike Race ..................8
4 – The Black Fly Challenge™ ..................13
5 – Ruined ..................17
6 – When Time Doesn't Fly ..................21
7 – Flying Up Uncas Road ..................23
8 – Ole' Jasper's Fly-Die ..................27
9 – How to Count the Animals ..................32
10 – On Your Mark. Get Set. Whoa! ...35
11 – The Puddle Club ..................39
12 – It's Lucy Calling ..................41
13 – The Blackfly Bad Guy ..................44
14 – Wails in the Woods ..................48
15 – Saved by the Bell ..................51
16 – On Common Ground ..................53
17 – Troubled Bridge Over Water ..................57
18 – A Daring Plan ..................61
19 – Bye-Bye Blackfly Bad Guy ..................65
20 – Pack Open – Case Closed ..................69
21 – Full Circle ..................75
Epilogue ..................80

"You still have your face painted?" Justin asked.
Nick smiled. "Why shouldn't I?"

## Chapter One

# What's All the BUZZ?

"How many riders do you think we'll get?" Justin Robert asked, struggling to spread out a small map on a short and stocky game table.

"Probably not many," Jackie Salsberry said, and reached out to help him. "Wait, fold the part of the map we don't need under itself and the section we want to look at should fit on the table perfectly."

It did.

Justin opened an aluminum lawn chair and sat down. "We'll need to get our own chairs to sit on this summer," he said. "All the ones in here go down by the dock." The cold metal bars of the seat against his legs made him shiver. "Right now we could use some kind of heater."

"What do you expect for early spring in the Adirondack mountains," Jackie said. She grabbed a chair and joined him. "Maybe this will take your mind off the cold. Let me show you our route for the race."

Justin didn't feel any warmer looking at the map, but Jackie was right. Working on their latest plan did take his mind off his chilly seat.

Every year a famous bicycle race, ***The Black Fly Challenge™***, took place in early June with a course running between Indian Lake and Jackie's home hamlet of Inlet.

Justin loved riding his bike and he knew the youngest person who ever entered and finished the challenge had been younger than he was. He had always wanted to take part in the race, and his dad was even going to take photographs for a magazine at this year's event. Still, he had to miss it.

"I think it's very cool your science project won first place," Jackie said, as she rotated the map her way for a better look at it. "You pick up your award that Saturday — and we'll do our own race on Sunday."

"Thanks again for figuring all this out," Justin said.

Jackie smiled. "No problem," she said, and lowered her finger to a point on the map. "We'll start the race right at this trailhead on the Uncas Road. From there we'll –

The door of the Roberts' storage cabin suddenly burst open, and a familiar voice rang out. "Are you guys in here?"

It was Nick Barnes from the camp next door, last in the trio of very best friends expected to attend the special meeting.

"Yes, we're here," Jackie said.

"You won't believe what happened!" Nick said.

Justin's calico cat, Dax, flashed between Nick's legs and beat him through the door.

Jackie didn't look up from the map. Neither did

Justin. They were both used to Nick's dramatic entrances. He was carrying a small box and set it on the floor.

"You guys!" Nick said. "This is serious!"

Dax jumped into Justin's lap. He smiled and worked his fingers into the white fur under her chin and down through her neck. Then he looked up at Nick. "You still have your face painted?" he said.

Nick smiled. "Why shouldn't I?" he said. "You're still wearing that Bug Lake shirt."

"But I didn't sleep in it!" Justin said.

Jackie remained focused on the map. "What is it, Nick?" she said. "What won't we believe?"

Nick took a long deep breath and slowly exhaled to calm himself down. "It's Bug-Eye," he said. "Bug-Eye is gone."

Jackie and Justin were silent. They looked at one another and then back at Nick.

"Don't you get it?" Nick said. "Bug-Eye, the giant blackfly that Justin rode on the carousel yesterday? Gone! Missing! Stolen!"

Nick was right.

They couldn't believe it.

## Chapter Two

# Bye-Bye Blackfly

"Bug-Eye was stolen?" Justin said. "Who would dare to try and take something that big with so many people around?"

"How do you even know it's gone?" Jackie said.

Nick was looking around the room. "Wow, you guys have already done a lot of work cleaning up this place," he said, and turning to Justin, bombarded him with questions. "Why are your parents letting us use the old storage cabin for a game room and library? What are we going to do with your kayaks? Hey, where are the washer and dryer? Oh, I'll bet they're up in the cabin now, right? It's so great you can come up here any time of year now that your parents turned your cabin into a camp for every season."

Nick finally took a breath and bent over to pick up the small box he had brought with him. It was filled with books. "So," he said. "Where are we going to put all these?"

"Nick," Jackie said firmly.

"What's wrong?" Nick said. "Isn't there going to be enough room to fit my books?"

Jackie sighed. "You just came running in here and made this big disturbing announcement that one of the carvings on the Adirondack Carousel was taken," she said. "Where did you get that terrible news?"

"Oh, my mom told me," Nick said. "One of her friends who knows one of the animal carvers called and told her. The police are pretty sure poor old Bug-Eye was taken sometime late last night."

Justin shook his head. "What a bad way for the carousel's birthday party to end," he said. "And who would even want to steal the blackfly? It's not like it was the cutest creature there. Why not take the deer or the raccoon or the eagle?"

Jackie challenged him. "Then why did you walk so fast to get ahead of everyone else and make a bee-line for the fly?" she said. "You were the first one in line. You had first pick of any animal you wanted to ride on the whole carousel."

Justin shrugged. "I don't know," he said. "I guess because —

"Because it was cool?" Jackie said.

"I guess so," Justin said.

Jackie nodded. "And that would also explain why you insisted on riding that not-so-cute blackfly three more times in a row," she said.

"Yeah," Nick said. "And right after I got my face painted, I saw this guy who kept trying to get a turn, but you kept beating him to it. He didn't look very happy about it, either."

Jackie paused, and looked at Justin. Her eyes

narrowed. "If we weren't with you the whole time to Saranac Lake and back again," she said, "I'd think you could be the thief."

Justin blushed. "That's not even funny," he said.

Nick squealed and dropped his box of books onto the game table. "I know who stole Bug-Eye!" he said.

Dax leaped to the floor and sought refuge in the bow of the red kayak.

Nick had the full attention of a startled Justin and Jackie.

"Who?" Justin said. Then he pushed at Jackie. "Because it wasn't me."

"Aliens!" Nick said.

Jackie lowered and shook her head. She even made a slight moan.

"Think about it," Nick said. "Bug-Eye even looks like an alien." He widened his own eyes for effect. "Maybe all the blackflies in the whole world are little aliens. That's why they chase people around and try to eat them."

Jackie reached into Nick's box of books. "Just what kind of crazy fiction have you been reading lately, anyway?" she said.

Nick ignored her. "And look at the way the carousel is shaped and keeps spinning around and around," he said. "I'll bet the whole thing is a flying saucer!"

That comment made it Jackie's turn to ignore Nick. She nudged Justin. "However that fly disappeared, there is one thing we do know," she said.

"What's that?" Justin said.

"You were the very last person to ride on Bug-Eye yesterday," Jackie said.

Nick disagreed. "You mean Justin was the very last human being to ride on Bug-Eye – ever," he said. "And I don't care what you two think. I'm telling you who came and took that fly. It was aliens."

## Chapter Three

# The Bug Lake Bike Race

Justin retrieved Dax from the kayak while Jackie removed Nick's box of books from the game table and set it back on the floor.

"Are we going to play a game now?" Nick asked.

"No," Justin said. "Jackie was just showing me the route she made up for our bike race."

"We're doing it the day after the blackfly race, right?" Nick said. "I love watching those gazillion bikes take off from the Inlet parking lot."

"Yes," Jackie said. "Now grab another chair and sit down with us."

The three friends gathered in a tight circle around the map on the game table with Dax at Justin's feet.

"Now that Nick is here, I think we need to make this official," Jackie said. She took a red marker from her pocket and carefully described the route that began at Uncas Road and ended at the Eighth Lake Campground. A trail of fresh ink appeared as her hand slowly moved across the map.

"That's a pretty long line," Nick said.

Jackie smiled and set the marker down. "Done," she said. "Now we can vote."

Nick protested. "But you used a big fat pen," he said. "If we don't like your route, it's too late to erase it."

Jackie smiled. "Exactly," she said.

"We also have to vote on the name of the race," Justin said. "Since we'll be going right by some of the Bug Lake shoreline I vote we call it, **The Bug Lake Bike Race**."

Again, Nick protested. "But you already made your homemade shirt with that name on it," he said.

Justin's smile was even bigger than Jackie's. "I know," he said.

Nick frowned. "Why do you two get to decide everything that's going to happen at the race, but I don't get to pick anything?" he said. "It's not fair."

"Okay," Jackie said. "We'll let you choose something."

"Really?" Nick said.

"Sure," Justin said. "Pick anything you want."

Jackie quickly shot Justin her famous look that said, *"what's-the-matter-with-you-are-you-crazy?"*

Nick smiled. "Anything?" he said.

Jackie grimaced. "Oh, no," she said, her eyes shut tight. "Here it comes."

"A scavenger hunt," Nick said.

Justin's eyes lit up. "That's a great idea," he said.

"It is?" Nick said.

Jackie was more cautious. "What kind of a scavenger hunt?" she asked.

"You know," Nick said. "The kind of scavenger hunt where you have to find neat stuff. Like gold coins and things like that. The one who finds the most riches wins."

"And where do you plan on finding gold coins while racing four miles on a bicycle through the woods?" Jackie said.

Nick swallowed hard. "Four miles?" he said. "We're racing four whole miles?"

"Would you rather race six-point-four kilometers?" Jackie said. "Which sounds better to you, riding four miles or six-point-four kilometers?"

"Four miles," Nick said. "I guess."

Justin whispered to Jackie. "But aren't six kilometers and four miles almost the same?"

Jackie smiled and winked. "Pretty close," she said. "I'm just trying to make four miles sound better."

"I heard that," Nick said. "If they're the same, then I'm going to tell people I raced all six-point-four calamities."

"Not calamities," Justin said. "Kilometers."

Jackie paused and gazed out the window. The lazy waves of Fourth Lake gently lapped against the rocky shore just a few feet from the storage cabin's front porch. "Maybe a scavenger hunt could be fun," she said.

"You said maybe," Nick said.

Justin smiled. "And you know what that means," he said.

"I know," Jackie said. "It means I say, yes."

Nick and Justin beamed.

"And in this case," Jackie continued, "it also means *I* get to decide exactly what we will search for in the hunt."

Nick and Justin looked at each other and shrugged.

"It's okay with me," Nick said.

"Fine with me, too," Justin said. He cleared his throat. "So, I vote we call our event, **The Bug Lake Bike Race**."

Jackie nodded. "And I vote we race six-point-four kilometers from the Uncas Road, past Bug Lake, to the Eighth Lake Campground."

Nick moaned.

"*All* six-point-four kilometers," Jackie said.

"Okay," Nick said. "And I vote while we race, we do a scavenger hunt."

"Good," Jackie said. "All in favor? Vote, 'Yes.'"

"Yes," Justin said.

"Yes," Nick said.

"I vote yes, too," Jackie said.

"*Meow*," said Dax from underneath the table.

Justin laughed. "Even Dax agrees," he said.

"So that makes it anonymous!" Nick said.

"*Unanimous*," Jackie said, correcting him. "We are all agreed and that makes it a *unanimous* decision."

Nick, who was always mixing up words, was already on to his next thought. "Wait a minute," he said. "What are we going to be looking for in the scavenger hunt?"

Jackie raised her eyebrows. "You'll find out a

week from next Sunday," she said. Then it was her turn to beam.

## Chapter Four

# The Black Fly Challenge™

Jackie felt bad when Nick called saying he had to miss the big race, too. **The Black Fly Challenge™** was born long before she was, but as far back as she could remember, she never missed a start.

The overcast day and slight drizzle did not dishearten the hundreds of racers who were already packed tightly in the town parking lot. Straddling their bikes, they were awaiting the crack of the starter pistol to release them all down the middle of Route 28 and on to the Moose River Plains.

Dozens of people lined both sides of the street, many of them poised to jump into their vehicles to make the drive to Indian Lake where they would meet the cyclists at the finish line.

Jackie knew the race was about to begin when one of the Inlet police officers stopped the traffic and Miss Carolyn, the official photographer, was setting up in her normal position. Outfitted in a blue rain slicker and wide-brimmed rain hat to help shield her equipment from the elements, she was stationed in front of the police car near the starting line on a

Jackie knew the race was about to begin
when Miss Carolyn, the official photographer,
was setting up in her normal position.

towering stepladder that was being kept steady by a volunteer.

Jackie knew an entire page of Miss Carolyn's photos along with a story would show up in the local newspaper, the *Weekly Adirondack*. That was why she surrendered her own traditional location in front of the Arrowhead Park sign for a spot closer to Miss Carolyn. Her hope was to catch the reporter before she left and ask her if she could take a picture at the finish of the Bug Lake race being held the next afternoon.

The announcements booming from a loudspeaker above the parking lot near the Information Center were few and the anxious riders were finally commanded to get ready.

There was a short hush and the only sound for a moment was the soft rain hitting the black pavement and then – ***Bang!*** – the cyclists took off.

"Some of these guys and gals will finish all 40 miles in two hours," Jackie heard a spectator say as the steady stream of colorful uniforms seemed to all blend together as they whisked by.

"It will take a few of them half the day!" another spectator said.

Jackie considered that as the riders continued to rush by in a blur. *40 miles,* she thought. *That's almost ten times the total distance of our race tomorrow.*

It seemed like the whirl of wheels whizzing by would never end, and then suddenly it was over. A few stragglers, those who had entered the race more for fun than to win any prize, struggled up the modest hill and finally out of sight.

Jackie was approaching Miss Carolyn to ask her about taking photos of the Bug Lake race, when one last cyclist suddenly burst from the mouth of the parking lot.

Wearing a backpack that appeared covered with flies, the wild rider swerved and darted between both Jackie and the photographer, nearly hitting both of them.

Stunned and watching the man speed up Route 28, more than his rude and erratic behavior struck Jackie as strange. He was also flying down the highway in the wrong direction!

## Chapter Five

# Ruined

Nick plopped down next to Justin and immediately began to whisper. "You're not going to believe this," he said.

Justin had expected Nick to be dropped off at the school. He just didn't know exactly when. Both of their mothers were in the parking lot, transferring his friend's belongings into the family Jeep for the weekend trip north.

Justin whispered back. "Now what happened?" he said. "Wait, don't tell me." He tried to compete with his overly dramatic friend. "Your mom just heard the whole carousel lifted off and flew into outer space!"

Nick frowned. "Worse than even that," he said. "Jackie totally ruined the scavenger hunt."

"Shhh!" The sound came from someone sitting behind them in the auditorium that was packed with parents and their children for the ***Camden Elementary Science Awards***.

Six teachers, one from each grade level, stood on the stage that was framed with blue velvet curtains and they were greeting each winner who stepped forward to receive his or her award. Alongside the teachers was a small table with the last few trophies to be presented.

"William Parker, would you kindly come forward, please?" announced Mrs. Sullivan from the podium.

Justin kept wondering why so many adults stopped talking normally when they were speaking in front of a large group of people – kind of like the pastor at his church did on Sunday mornings.

It wasn't often the younger children from the elementary school visited the huge high school facility and the young boy in the front row slowly rose from his seat and made his way up the small flight of stairs to the stage.

Justin thought his poor classmate looked less like someone collecting a trophy and more like someone who thought he was in trouble and was walking to the principal's office.

Mrs. Sullivan continued. "William has taken first place with his project, *The Spitting Volcano*," she said. "Congratulations, William."

There was polite applause and a few whistles.

Nick took full advantage of the noise from the crowd to speak to Justin again. "We're not hunting for gold coins. Not even colored rocks or stones or any kind of good treasure at all," he said. "We should never have voted to let Jackie choose."

Justin disagreed. "I'm sorry you're mad because your dad had to work and you're missing the black-fly race today, but you shouldn't take it out on Jackie," he said. "At least we get to ride to camp together this afternoon and do our own race tomorrow."

Nick persisted. "I talked to Jackie just before we left to come here, so I know this is true," he said. "Don't you even want to know what she's going to have us looking for in the scavenger hunt?"

The next announcement came quickly. "Joanna March. Would you come forward for your award? Joanna has won for her project, *Dinosaur Bones in the Stones*."

Far from shy, the spunky third grader nearly stumbled as she launched like a missile from her seat and hustled up the stairs to collect her prize. There was more handclapping.

Justin scolded Nick. "We'll have to talk later," he said. "I don't want to miss when my name is called."

"You have to hear this," Nick said. "Jackie wants each of us to carry some kind of camera. Then while we're racing we're supposed to stop and take pictures of toads and insects and things like that. See what I mean? She ruined it. She also told me only five other people even signed up for the race. Can you blame them? Who would want to do a scavenger hunt and just chase around some stupid old butterflies?"

"Justin Robert," Mrs. Sullivan said, "would you come forward now to receive your award?" She paused. "It is my distinct honor to announce Justin has won the grand prize for his beautiful and extraordinary science project, *Butterflies and Moths of the Adirondacks*."

As the audience erupted into spontaneous applause, Nick sank into his chair and tried to disappear.

## Chapter Six

# When Time Doesn't Fly

It was particularly difficult for Justin to sit through the church service Sunday morning. Everything was laid out at camp ready and waiting for him. That way he could quickly slip out of his formal clothes and into his outfit for the race.

He pictured the items in their exact location, reviewing each one in checklist fashion.

Sitting on his bed on the sleeping porch were his sweatshirt, a short-sleeve shirt, pants, bucket hat, head net and helmet. Borrowed from his dad was a small digital camera with fresh AA batteries, along with special mesh gloves to help protect his hands from those little flying vampires.

The gloves were stuffed where he knew he could not forget them, into his unlaced boots resting on the floor.

His bicycle with tires freshly pumped full of air was propped by a kickstand in the driveway and pointed in the direction of Uncas Road.

He had also discovered a clever way to attach an Adirondack pack basket to the handlebars – the perfect place to carry a liter of water and for Dax to hitch a ride.

Yes. Everything was there. All ready. All waiting.

Justin kept glancing out the window to check on the weather. It was overcast and leaves were slightly moving.

He knew the easy breeze coupled with the local fly control program would help keep the number of blackflies at bay – at least in the hamlet. What he couldn't know for sure is what the blackfly population might be like on the trail.

He would probably be okay if he kept moving. But what about when he stopped to take photographs for the scavenger hunt in the middle of the woods? He felt itchy and began scratching at his arms and legs just thinking about the possibilities.

Following the closing hymn at the end of the service, Justin stood at the back of the church trying to wait patiently while his parents said their farewells to friends.

That was when he overheard Mrs. Chambers behind him speaking to the pastor at the door.

"The word is out that every banner in Inlet for the blackfly race is missing," he heard her say.

The pastor shook his head. "Who would even want to do something like that?" he said. "Do they think it was children? A prank?"

"Well, if it was a prank, no one thinks it's funny," Mrs. Chambers said. "Even the local police are investigating now."

## Chapter Seven

# Flying Up Uncas Road

Once he was home from church and with everything so well prepared, it only took Justin a few minutes to change his clothes, hop on his bike and speed across the quiet highway toward the trailhead on Uncas Road.

His calico cat, Dax, who liked to hide in everything from small boxes to gym bags, felt right at home in the large Adirondack pack basket. She stood on her hind legs and Justin thought she seemed to really be enjoying the ride and the view.

He knew his parents were already loading the family Jeep with supplies for the special picnic that would be waiting for all the cyclists at the Eighth Lake Campground upon completion of the race.

Justin also knew Jackie and Nick planned to arrive at the trailhead ahead of everyone else. Nick had called him from her house where he had stayed overnight to tell him Jackie had decided not to compete, but would be race organizer and make sure everyone would be safe and accounted for on the trail.

Pedaling with great vigor, he still wondered if he

might be late, but that fear disappeared as he rounded a bend in the road and saw two bicycles not far ahead of him.

No sooner had he overtaken the two racers and learned their names, when the roar of a vehicle from behind convinced all of them it would be safest to pull over and stop.

The boy with the red-and-white bike, Aiden, appeared intimidated by the professional-looking mountain bike he saw hanging on the rack on the back of the white Suburban zooming by. "I sure hope whoever owns that bike won't be in the race," he said.

The girl with the black-and-gold bike next to him, Addison, was totally unimpressed. "It doesn't matter who owns that bike," she said. "Like it said on the sign-up sheet, there's more to this race than riding."

Justin was surprised at how aggressive Addison was with the younger boy. It seemed a little bold to talk that way with someone you had just met. He gulped when she suddenly turned his way and he braced himself for what she might say to him.

"You'll have to pardon my little brother," Addison said. "He's afraid of everything."

"Oh!" Justin said, and noticed their similar round faces and dark-brown eyes. "Aiden's your brother!"

As they remounted their bicycles and continued up the road, Aiden sought to defend himself. "I am not afraid of everything," he said to his sister. "And stop calling me little."

"Well, you are little," Addison said. "And you are

afraid." She looked over at Justin. "Of ev-er-y-thing."

There was very little conversation after that as they travelled along.

Justin did learn the two siblings were from Rochester, New York. They made many weekend trips to Old Forge and Inlet and usually spent two weeks every summer in Lake Placid.

The road had turned from pavement to dirt and Justin knew they were close to their destination.

The white Suburban zoomed back by them, and Aiden winced when he looked back and discovered the mountain bike was missing from the rack.

Addison saw the look on her brother's face and laughed.

Justin noticed the license plate instead. It was a solid green – the same color as their storage cabin – and from the design, he recognized it immediately as being from the neighboring state of Vermont. *Wow*, he thought. *We're getting racers from everywhere.*

Justin could hear voices ahead. It was around the next bend in the road he recognized Jackie with the racers, sharing the modest parking space with a pick-up truck directly across from the trailhead.

As he and Aiden and Addison parked their bikes, he grimaced.

An awful odor had immediately assaulted his nose, making his eyes water. Dax had even begun to sneeze.

*It's not a skunk*, Justin thought. *Or maybe it's decayed leaves that were uncovered by the recently melted snow.*

Then he realized what everyone who had been there for a few moments already knew.

The horrible smell?

It was Nick.

## Chapter Eight

# Ole' Jasper's Fly-Die

Jackie gathered the six cyclists and two parents who were present into a small semi-circle in front of her. "Do we all know each other yet?" she said, and glanced at her clipboard. "I'm Jackie, and I think everyone already knows Nick."

There were some polite nods among the group.

Addison wasn't shy. "I'm Addison, but you can call me Addie," she said. "And I'm here with my little brother, Aiden."

Aiden was not happy being introduced by his sister as little, but still gave a quick wave.

Justin introduced himself as Jackie's friend. "Oh, yes," he said. "And this is my cat, Dax."

There was a collective sigh as, on cue, the calico popped her head from the top of the pack basket. "She'll be riding with me," Justin said.

"She is so pretty," said the only other girl rider. "Can I pet her?"

"Sure," Justin said.

There was a collective sigh from
everyone as, on cue, Dax popped her head
from the top of the pack basket.

“Tell everyone your name,” one of the adults said to the young girl. Justin figured it was her father.

“My name is Mattie,” she said, and gently stroked Dax’s head. “I love to ride my bike.”

“This is Mattie’s first ride on a trail like this and her first race,” her mother offered. “We are a little nervous, but very excited.”

Mattie smiled at her. “Don’t worry, Mom,” she said. “I’ll be okay.”

Addison leaned toward Justin, and whispered. “I think that girl might have that Down thing,” she said.

Justin shrugged. “I know,” he said. “It’s called Down Syndrome.”

“But how will she ride a bike?” Addison said. “Isn’t that like – impossible?”

Justin laughed. “Not if she’s anything like this girl at our school who plays soccer,” he said. “Nothing ever seems to stop her from doing whatever she wants to do.”

Aiden kept staring at the last rider who had yet to be introduced. It was the boy with the fancy mountain bike. The bike he had seen on the back of the white Suburban!

Dressed like a professional racer in a spandex shirt and pants, the older boy stopped fussing with the gears and wheels of his cycle only long enough to flatly state his name, where he was from, and why he was there.

“I’m R.J.,” the tall boy said, strapping his helmet on over a mop of long blonde hair. “I’m from New

Jersey, but I'm here with my grandparents who live in Vermont. I was supposed to be in the big race yesterday, but my grandfather thought it started at Indian Lake and we got here too late."

Jackie looked at her clipboard. "So you are Ryan Jones," she said, and checked off his name on the sheet.

"R.J. from NJ," Nick said. "That's easy to remember."

"Well, everyone, here are your maps," Jackie said, and began to pass them out. "I've put them in clear plastic sandwich bags to help keep them protected and dry."

"Are there sandwiches in there, too?" Nick said. "I'll have a peanut butter and jelly."

"No, Nick," Jackie said. "There will be hamburgers and hot dogs waiting at the picnic area where we finish the race at the campground. Now let me explain how the scavenger hunt is going to work."

"I'm not doing that part," R.J. said. "I'm racing straight through."

"That's fine," Jackie said. "But first, hear all the rules." She pointed and whispered something to Nick as she handed him the last map.

Nick blurted a response. "Why do I have to move way over there?" he said. "I won't be able to hear any of the rules."

Jackie shot right back at him, but in a controlled manner and with authority. "I would like you to move, Nick Barnes," she said, "because your smell is disgusting. And if you insist on standing right here no one will hear any of the rules, because you're about to make me gag."

Nick frowned and stomped several feet away. Then he turned back toward Jackie and took a defiant stance with his arms crossed. "I got this recipe from one of my grandpa's old guidebooks," he said. "It's called, **Ole' Jasper's Fly-Die**, and it works."

That was when Justin noticed a clear, thick goop that was indeed smeared all over Nick's face, neck and hands. He also noticed that a few blackflies were actually stuck to Nick's forehead and cheeks – some with wings still buzzing in a futile attempt to escape. He wondered how the noise of the ones trapped and struggling near his ears weren't driving him crazy. But he had to admit his friend was right. Other than the ones that were stuck to Nick's fly-die, there wasn't another blackfly yet in sight.

## Chapter Nine

# How to Count the Animals

"Reptiles, amphibians, mammals, birds, arthropods." Jackie listed all the different creatures the riders should be on the lookout for during the scavenger hunt.

Nick asked a question most of the other kids were thinking. "What's an arthropod?" he asked. "It sure sounds like robots or aliens to me."

"I know what they are," Justin said. He remembered from his science project. "Things like butterflies and centipedes and spiders."

Nick grinned. "Spiders?" he said. He knew Jackie was afraid of them.

Jackie quickly moved along. "If you happen to see a mammal, don't try to get near it," she said. "You'll get one point for every different animal you take a photograph of, and an extra point for every one of them you can call by its correct name."

Aiden looked worried. "Do you think there will be any bears?" he said.

"It's not likely," Jackie said. "Animals usually hear and see you before you hear and see them, and they normally try to avoid contact with humans."

Aiden did not appear comforted by her words.

"And remember," Jackie said. "If you happen to see more than one of the same animal, you can only count one of them."

"What do you win if you're the first one across the finish line?" R.J. said.

"The person who finishes the race first will get six extra points," Jackie said. She looked at R.J. "But it is very possible to finish the course in first place but still not have enough points to win the race."

Aiden raised his hand. "The poster we saw said the winner gets some tickets to ride a carousel," he said. "Is that the place on your sweatshirt?"

"Yes, it is," Jackie said. "The winner will receive four tickets to ride the Adirondack Carousel in Saranac Lake."

"And it is awesome!" Nick said. "I rode the loon called Lucy! All the animals on the carousel have names."

Jackie smiled. "Actually, many of the creatures that are on the carousel are also those you might even see on the trail today."

Addison poked Aiden. "I'll bet there's even a bear on it," she said.

"There is a bear," Nick said. "Its name is Paws."

Aiden frowned. He didn't think his sister was funny – at all.

"Hey, someone's coming up the road," Justin said. "She looks familiar."

"Oh, good," Jackie said. "It's Grace. She goes to

my school and said she might come to help out. Are there any other questions before she gets here?"

"Yes," R.J. said. "When are we going to start this race?"

*Ring-ring. Ring-ring. Ring-ring.* Mattie was already on her bike and her busy thumb was pushing the lever on the metal ringer bell that looked like a ladybug.

Jackie looked at her watch. "Perfect," she said. "Everybody line up. **The Bug Lake Bike Race** begins right now!"

## Chapter Ten

# On Your Mark. Get Set. Whoa!

As the racers walked their bicycles across the road to line up at the trailhead, Jackie approached Justin. "Can I keep my clipboard in your pack basket?" she asked.

Justin nodded, and as she carefully slipped the board into the basket behind Dax, he whispered. "I've been wanting to tell you," he said. "I found out this morning all the banners in town for the blackfly race were taken last night."

"That's not all that's been stolen," Jackie said.

Justin was surprised. "There's more?" he said.

*Ring-ring. Ring-ring.* Mattie's thumb was working her bell, an alert that everyone was in position and ready to go. And the only thing in the group brighter than her pink-and-white bike was her smile.

R.J. was in front, still examining his mountain bike for any possible problems.

Addison and Aiden were behind him, side by side.

And Grace was helping Mattie adjust her bright pink helmet, assuring her parents it was fine for them to leave for the campground where the race would end.

It appeared no one wanted to ride behind Nick, who was saturated with **Ole' Jasper's Fly-Die**. He was the last in line.

"Sorry, Justin, we'll have to talk later," Jackie said. "I have to get this race started." She hustled across the road with her own bike, joining Grace and Mattie in line, and quickly described the terrain the group would cover.

The trail would run up and down. It would be narrow in places and wide in others. Some stretches would be flat and smooth, but rocks and roots along the way were more common. They would also be crossing several short wooden bridges and at one point have an open view of Bug Lake.

"Follow the yellow trail markers and take your time," Jackie said. "**The Bug Lake Bike Race** is not simply about speed! It's about enjoying all you can see along the way."

At this particular moment, all Justin could see was one spot left to line up, and it was next to Nick. He pulled out the head net that was stashed in the pocket of his pants and draped it over the extra large bucket hat that sat on top of his snug helmet.

The net covered his face and neck and dropped all the way to his shoulders. He knew it would protect him from any blackflies, but he hoped it might also help buffer the terrible odor. Slightly holding his breath, he rolled up next to his friend and stopped.

Nick laughed. "You look like an alien," he said. "You look like an alien bee keeper!" He started to slip off his backpack. "I've got a whole jar full of **Fly-Die** in here. Let me give you some and you can take that net off your head and not look so weird."

Justin stared at Nick and wondered if the smell from **Ole' Jasper's** gel had done something to his brain. Nick's face was peppered with dead blackflies and he thought that the head net made *him* look weird?

Jackie's next announcement commanded their attention and Nick readjusted his backpack. "Too late now, Justin," he said.

"I'm fine with my net," Justin said.

"All right, Mattie," Jackie said. "The next time you ring your bell, we'll start."

There was not a split second of further delay.

*Ring-ring. Ring-ring.* Mattie's bell sounded and the racers were off.

All except Justin, who was sure he saw something strange moving in the road.

An Eastern Tiger Swallowtail landed near Justin and he tried to snap a picture of it.

## Chapter Eleven

# The Puddle Club

It was suddenly very quiet.

Mattie's parents had driven away and the last of the racers quickly melted into the woods.

Justin leaned his bike against a tree and took the small camera from his pack basket. "Wait here, Dax," he said.

Distracted by all the initial excitement, he now took time to concentrate on his surroundings. Walking slowly toward the movement he saw in the road, he noticed while there were not yet many blackflies in the air, there were some butterflies. Tiger Swallowtails to be exact, and there were lots of them.

One landed near him, and he tried to sneak up on it for a picture. It quickly darted away and he followed it toward that spot where, as he got closer, it appeared a section of the road itself was moving.

He stopped short and caught his breath when he realized what he had found.

It was a puddle club.

A mass of Tiger Swallowtails – he figured there had to be nearly one hundred – were gathered together in the moist dirt where a shallow puddle had formed from the previous day's rain and was nearly dried up.

There were so many of them, their yellow and black wings gently fanning in slow motion, it was almost impossible to tell where one butterfly ended and another began.

But he did know from his science project what was happening. The butterflies had flown into a little roadside diner and were sucking up all the salts and minerals that had drained and collected there.

Justin was so excited he almost forgot to take a picture. He was happy to find he could get quite close without startling them. It wasn't easy to peer through the mesh of the head net, but he managed to snap several shots with his camera and then slowly backed away.

He smiled. "That's already two points," he said out loud, softly talking to himself. "One point for the butterfly, and one point because I know exactly what it's named."

He heard Mattie's bell ring. The sound was faint, and he knew everyone had already travelled quite a distance along the trail.

Sprinting back to his bike, he found Dax curled up and asleep in the bottom of the pack basket.

"Sorry, girl," Justin said, as the jarring movement of the bike woke her up. "We have to get moving."

## Chapter Twelve

# It's Lucy Calling

What would be the best way for him to win those tickets to ride the carousel? That's the question that was on Nick's mind.

At first he thought it would be best to move hard and fast. After all, he had already successfully pedaled past everyone but R.J. from NJ.

And that was Nick's big problem. He didn't know how far the boy on his fancy bike was ahead of him, but he did know the muscles in his own legs were beginning to burn and there was no way he would ever catch up to him.

Nick hated to admit it, but he finally decided Jackie's strategy would give him the best chance to win the race. He must slow down and take some pictures of animals for some points.

That made him wonder how many creatures he had already missed. He had seen Addison and Aiden with bikes parked and kneeling with their cameras over something they must have spotted on a rotting log.

And how many points might Mattie have? She had

both Grace and Jackie to help her. He had passed the three of them way back near the junction for Black Bear Mountain. When he saw them, they were moving along, single file, with Mattie between Grace and Jackie and still ringing her bell.

All he knew about Justin was that he was somewhere far behind everybody — maybe even had a flat tire.

Nick moaned. His legs were spent, and for some relief he removed his feet from the pedals. This allowed him to straighten his legs and he coasted down a small hill until his bicycle slowly came to rest all on its own.

Standing while straddling his bike in the middle of the trail, he heard a haunting cry from somewhere in the woods.

"A Common Loon," Nick said. "I must be near Bug Lake!" Because he also knew the correct name of the bird he thought, *if I can get a picture of a loon, then that would be two points!*

Something bumped his boot. "A toad!" he said. Forgetting his achy legs, he jumped off his bike, grabbed his camera and knelt down to take a picture.

The toad seemed to know when Nick was about to snap a shot, because just as he clicked the shutter, it hopped away.

"Calm down, Buck," he said, remembering that was the name of the toad on the carousel. "Don't be camera shy!" It took three tries, but he was finally successful.

The excitement of securing his first point encouraged him to walk, rather than ride, his bicycle forward and scan the ground for any more creeping, crawling creatures that could bring him even more points.

*A salamander*, he thought. *Or maybe a spider*. He liked that idea because he knew Jackie would jump if he showed her a picture of any creature with eight or more legs. Maybe she would even award him with extra points if he promised he *wouldn't* show her a picture of a spider!

He heard the loon again. It sounded much closer this time.

That was when Nick noticed the distinct impression of bicycle tire tracks in some soft dirt that veered off the main trail to his left. Upon closer inspection, he realized the tracks were actually embedded in an unmarked trail, the overgrown pathway barely recognizable.

Nick wondered if R.J. from NJ had changed his mind and decided not to race straight through to the campground. Maybe he had the same plan as Nick and decided to head toward the call of the loon. Multiple tracks appeared to indicate a bicycle had gone both up the trail and back out again.

Nick had another decision to make. Should he also see if the trail led to Bug Lake and try to get a picture of the loon? Or should he stick to the main trail and keep moving forward?

The loon called again.

"Okay, Lucy," Nick said. "I'm coming."

## Chapter Thirteen

# The Blackfly Bad Guy

Nick was glad he had left his bike hidden behind a large boulder near the start of the narrow pathway. The unmarked trail started out friendly enough – soft, flat and smooth. But very quickly it rose and morphed into bare rock that was cracked and crumbling.

With camera in hand and pack on his back, Nick hiked the rough and ever-upward path until it suddenly opened into a clearing that was bordered with a few trees. It was a quaint campsite and was located right next to the water.

"Bug Lake!" Nick said. He took a few more steps and stopped.

A one-man tent with an unobstructed view of the lake was pitched near a fire pit that was littered with cooking utensils.

A hooded red sweatshirt with the word WISCONSIN printed on the front was draped over a low branch and a large piece of white canvas was spread out and lying near the tent on the ground.

No one appeared to be around and Nick hustled to the shoreline to scan the lake for any sign of the loon. "Come on, Lucy, where are you?" he said.

The loon did call, but this time from far off.

There was a cool breeze and Nick could barely make out the bird's head and long neck that appeared and then disappeared as its body bobbed up and down in the choppy water. He sighed, knowing the loon would only be a teeny speck in any picture he tried to take. But he raised his camera and took one anyway.

Walking further along the shoreline, he noticed several dragonflies hovering above some lush vegetation. One landed on top of a rust-colored rock and *snap*, Nick had taken another picture to secure point number four.

The silence was broken with the clicking of footsteps on bare rock.

Nick turned expecting to see the camper, but it was a deer. He held his breath and knelt down in some tall grass as the doe moved cautiously toward the center of the campsite. She looked behind her, and that's when a second tiny deer with white specks on its back entered Nick's view – a fawn – making its way on wobbly legs toward its mother.

Nick raised his camera and *snap* – mother and baby deer – both captured in the same picture! He began to take another shot when the doe froze, its nose pointed into the air. The deer looked his way, and he lowered his head, hoping to escape her gaze.

"Please don't go," he whispered, sure her sudden alarm was caused by the click from his camera.

His plea went unanswered. Daring to peer out again

The deer looked Nick's way, and he lowered
his head, hoping to escape her gaze.

between the blades of grass that was his hiding place, both deer were gone.

But he also discovered why they had left, and it wasn't something he had done at all.

Taking the place of the deer at the center of the campsite was a young man who had quickly dismounted a bicycle that appeared even fancier than R.J.'s.

Nick was about to rise and walk forward to introduce himself, when he saw the man bend over to pick up the large piece of canvas that was lying on the ground. The material may have been blank on one side, but it sure wasn't blank on the other side.

Awkward for one person to manage it, especially when swatting at a swarm of attacking blackflies at the same time, the man struggled in an attempt to brush the canvas off and roll it up.

As the stiff fabric flapped in the breeze and twisted in the man's hands, Nick recognized what it was. It was a giant banner. And on the front of the banner were the words written in bold red and blue lettering: *Ride The Black Fly Challenge.*

## Chapter Fourteen

# Wails in the Woods

As Justin cycled along a flat and narrow stretch of the trail that was flanked by budding ferns, he was thinking his chances of winning the race were pretty good.

Not only had he managed to pass by everyone except Nick and R.J., which put him close to the lead, but he had also collected photographs of a salamander and a young porcupine that had inched its way up a short tree right alongside the path.

Dax had helped him find the salamander, which was hiding under some dead leaves.

And it was while taking a picture of the porcupine when on the same tree a brown bird with a buffy breast landed on a branch right in front of him. A Hermit Thrush! Justin recognized it as the bird Jackie had ridden on the carousel. If he hadn't had his camera already lifted and poised for the porcupine, he never would have captured the shot. But just before the bird flew off, he got it!

Added together with his picture of the Tiger Swallowtails, Justin could not imagine anyone would have more points than he did. That is, no one except maybe Mattie who was being helped by Jackie, the nature expert among them all.

Now Justin was after a loon.

He had heard the bird's call off in the distance earlier, but hoped when he reached the spot he had seen on the map where the trail met the shoreline of the lake, he might actually have a clear view of it.

"Did you hear that, Dax?" Justin said to his calico. She still seemed to be enjoying the ride through the woods. "That loon is getting louder and louder."

The idea that he might actually get a picture of a loon made Justin's insides tickle, like he had a stomach full of buzzing blackflies.

Anxious to get to the lake, he was frustrated that again he had to dismount his bike at the bottom of another small hill. The combined weight of Dax, along with everything else in the pack basket, made the upward climb on wheels impossible.

As Justin crested the hill, he was stunned to find someone at the top straddling his bike to greet him. "R.J.?" he said. "I thought for sure you would already be at the campground."

The loon called again.

"Wait," R.J. said. Then he whispered. "Did you hear that?"

Justin nodded. That's when he could tell the eerie sound of the loon had R.J. petrified.

"I've been hearing it for quite a while," R.J. said. There was a slight quiver in his voice, and he kept peering into the woods. "I think it might be a wolf."

Justin recalled the fear he felt the very first time he heard the haunting tremolos and wails of a Common Loon. He was tempted to leave the rude boy behind, but quickly replaced that shameful thought with an act of mercy.

"It's a loon," Justin said.

"A loon?" R.J. said. He looked confused. Then his back straightened and his tone became bold and hard again, almost angry. "You mean it's just a bird?"

"Well, it's a pretty cool bird," Justin said. "I'm surprised you never heard any loons when you visited your grandparents in Vermont."

R.J. was no longer interested in any conversation. Lurching his bike forward, he stuck his toes back into the rattrap pedals of his bike and sped off.

Justin called after him. "Hey, wait," he said. "Have you seen Nick?"

"No!" R.J. called back sharply. "And I haven't smelled him either."

## Chapter Fifteen

# Saved by the Bell

Nick was puzzled. *Why would a guy in the woods have the blackfly banner from Arrowhead Park*, he wondered. His pounding heart seemed to be warning him to remain hidden and backtrack to his bike as silently and quickly as possible.

Slowly attempting his retreat, Nick stiffened as the man with the banner sneezed, rubbed his nose and peered in his direction. It seemed **Ole' Jasper's Fly-Die** kept away blackflies, but not necessarily camp guys.

Nick didn't even realize he was holding his breath until the man resumed his battle with the flies and the banner. Half crawling and half running he hurried his panicked soul back to the unmarked trail and once there did not stop sprinting until he reached the boulder concealing his bike.

The muscles in Nick's legs were no longer stiff and even if they still had been, it was doubtful he would have noticed.

Rushing toward the main trail, he leapt onto his

bike like a cowboy jumping onto his horse in a western movie get-away.

Nick's legs then churned with a frenzy, making the whirling wheels begin to sing. It didn't take long, however, before his muscles became weary again, and he knew he could not keep up such a frantic pace.

More than anything else Nick longed to be with his friends. The burden of the information he was harboring in his chest seemed ten times heavier than the weight he was carrying in his backpack. Something about that camper was not right, and he simply could not wait to unload everything he was feeling on Justin and Jackie.

*Keep pedaling*, he told himself. *Keep on pedaling*. And he did. Until he reached another steep incline and simply lost the strength to ride any further.

He considered his immediate surroundings, looking for some wide trees or another large boulder. *I'll just hide and rest in the woods awhile*, he thought.

And that's when he heard it.

*Ring-ring. Ring-ring.*

Nick smiled.

Saved by the bell!

## Chapter Sixteen

# On Common Ground

The sound of Mattie's ringer bell renewed Nick's resolve to push on. He forced his bicycle forward and rode until a short distance ahead he recognized a bright pink helmet in sharp contrast to the surrounding spring greenery.

Standing with Grace and Jackie, Mattie had stopped ringing her bell. All of their bikes were parked at the only open spot where the main trail ran directly alongside the Bug Lake shoreline.

Nick's heart leaped when he noticed a fourth parked bike and realized Justin was with them. He jumped from his own bike while it was rolling and laid it down while still on the run, dashing for the safety of the group. Breathless and with chest heaving, he managed to exhale a name. "Jackie," he said.

"Shhh," Jackie said. She pointed to Justin who was standing with his camera on a slab of rock that extended into the water like a small peninsula.

"Lucy?" Nick said.

The Common Loon had surfaced just a few feet

from shore, and Justin was getting a perfect photo for the scavenger hunt.

"We took some pictures, too," Jackie said.

Nick reached for his camera. "Then it's my turn," he said.

The wail of a loon sounded from somewhere across the water, and the bird in front of Justin disappeared, as if the lake itself had just swallowed it up.

"There are two loons out there?" Nick said. "And I didn't even get one picture."

Jackie asked Grace if she could continue up the trail with Mattie. "Addison and Aiden shouldn't be far ahead," she said. "We'll catch up with you in a minute."

Grace nodded, and she and Mattie and the ringing bell were on their way.

"Are you sure Addison and Aiden are ahead of us, too?" Nick said.

"Yes, we're all ahead of you, Nick Barnes," an unhappy Jackie said, firmly pressing her index finger into his chest. "Where have you been?"

Justin walked up to their friend, but was a bit gentler than Jackie. "We were worried about you, Nick," he said. "I caught up to R.J., and even he hadn't seen you."

"That's what I was trying to tell you," Nick said. "I heard the loon and found an unmarked trail to the lake, and that's when I saw this guy –

"You found an unmarked trail?" Justin said.

"Wait a minute," Jackie said. "I know about that trail. You saw what guy there?"

The Common Loon surfaced
just a few feet from the shore.

Nick shrugged. "He was just a camper," he said. "I don't know why, but I got kind of scared when I saw that he was trying to roll up the blackfly banner from the tennis court in the park."

Justin and Jackie looked at one another and their eyes widened.

Nick noticed their surprise. "What?" he said.

Jackie took him by the shoulders. "You are absolutely, positively sure it was the banner from the park for the blackfly race?" she said.

"I'm sure of it," Nick said. "Why?"

"Because," Justin said, "it means you might have found the blackfly bad guy."

## Chapter Seventeen

# Troubled Bridge Over Water

"Both blackfly banners were taken last night?" Nick said. "Even the one over the highway?"

The three friends were racing single file to catch up with the rest of the group. Jackie was in the lead. "That's right," she said. "And it rained pretty hard yesterday afternoon. If he had the banner that was taken from the tennis court laying on the ground, I would guess he was trying to get it dried out."

"I knew there was something wrong going on," Nick said. "I just knew it."

Justin and Dax were last in line. He called ahead to Jackie. "Way back at the trailhead you started to tell me some other things were taken," he said.

"There were a lot of things taken from the Information Center," Jackie said. "Even an expensive jersey that was made special just for this year's race."

"It's like almost anything in town that had the word blackfly on it disappeared," Justin said.

"And now we know who is probably to blame," Jackie said.

"We've got to let your parents know before that guy gets away," Nick said.

One of the last wooden bridges of the main trail was just ahead and they could see Mattie and Grace, along with Addison and Aiden, had stopped just short of crossing over it.

As they drew closer, Jackie recognized the sign for the Seventh Lake lean-to that featured a drawing of a bear riding a bicycle. Nailed to two trees, it was not only a trail sign, but was also a sign to Jackie they still had a good amount of distance yet to cover. She looked back over her shoulder at Nick and Justin. "Let me handle this," she said. "There's no reason to worry anyone else in the group."

Aiden was waving and grinning as the trio pulled up alongside them. "I got a picture of a toad," he said.

"We have to get going right now," Nick said. There was a sense of urgency in his voice.

Aiden's grin disappeared. He looked up at Nick. "What's wrong?" he said.

Addison poked her brother and pointed to the sign above them nailed between the trees. "I told you that's what it's for," she said. "There must be a bear coming."

Aiden's eyes became wet with tears. "There is?" he said.

Jackie glared at Nick, then turned to Aiden and smiled. "There are no bears," she assured the young boy. "And congratulations on finding that toad! But we won't have time to stop for any more pictures for the scavenger hunt, or we'll be late for the picnic."

She slapped a blackfly that had landed on her hand. "That's my first one today. I don't know about the rest of you, but it looks like my bug repellant has lost most of its power."

Justin's head felt heavy and sweaty from wearing the helmet and bucket hat and head net, but other than Nick, he was the only other one not suddenly swinging away at blackflies.

"I still have plenty of **Ole' Jasper's** left if anyone wants some," Nick said.

The awkward silence that followed Nick's offer was interrupted by Mattie's ringer bell, which for that moment sounded as a dinner bell. "I am hungry," she said. "Let's go to the picnic."

Jackie suggested Grace and Mattie set the pace, while Addison, Aiden and Nick followed in the middle. She and Justin would remain in the back. "Eagles Nest Lake is just ahead and then it's on to the campground," she said.

*Ring-ring. Ring-ring*. "And the picnic," Mattie said.

Jackie laughed. "Yes," she said. "And the picnic."

With the group members laughing and chatting among themselves as they cycled forward, Justin held Jackie back for a moment. The two of them stood across from each other, still straddling their bikes at the center of the bridge. Jackie's bike was pointed back toward Uncas Road and Justin's forward, toward the campground.

"What is it, Justin?" Jackie asked. She slapped at another blackfly. "Where are all these flies coming from so suddenly?"

Justin hesitated before speaking. "I was just thinking," he said. "If that blackfly guy was trying to roll up the banner like Nick said, do you think he was getting ready to pack up and leave his camp?"

Jackie's eyes grew wide. "I'm pretty sure that is exactly what he was doing," she said.

Justin saw the startled look on her face. "How do you know that for sure?" he said.

"Come on," Jackie said. She turned her bike around and hit her pedals so hard the back tire spun in place and actually left a rubber mark on one of the bridge's wooden planks. "We have to go."

"Wait," Justin said. "What's wrong? How do you know that guy was packing to leave?"

"I know," Jackie said, "because I'm positive it's him coming down the trail behind us – right now!"

## Chapter Eighteen

# A Daring Plan

Jackie was barking out orders as she and Justin flew along the trail. "We'll never outrun him with Mattie and Aiden," she said. "We'll just try to keep everybody ahead of him for as long as we can."

Justin dared to look back over his shoulder. "He's not riding too fast," he said. "He's wearing a pack that looks like it's pretty heavy."

"It's probably heavy, all right," Jackie said, "especially if it's filled with everything that's missing from town!"

As the two of them caught up with the group, Grace called back to Jackie. "We're going to find a place to rest soon," she said. "Mattie and Aiden are a little bit tired."

"No problem," Jackie said. "I'll find a good place."

Justin pushed a whisper. "What are we going to do, Jackie?" he said, and looked back again. "I don't see him yet, but if we keep going this slow he'll catch us for sure."

The trail slightly widened.

"I've got an idea," Jackie said.

Justin dared to look back at the rider behind them. "He's not moving too fast," he said. "He's wearing a heavy pack."

Justin watched as Jackie passed by everyone to say something to Grace who had taken the lead. He saw Grace nod and then Jackie slowed down, allowing everyone to pass by her until she was alongside him again. "What's going on?" he said. "What did you tell Grace?"

"Okay, here's the plan," Jackie said. "Pretty soon we'll be coming to a junction. This trail keeps going straight to the campground. But there is also a left turn on the unmarked Eagles Nest Lake trail."

Justin's eyes brightened. "I get it," he said. "We'll all turn left, and the blackfly guy will go right by and miss all of us."

"Well, *they* will turn left," Jackie said. "I told Grace that she and Nick should rest the group there, but that you and I will keep going and ride as fast as we can to the campground to let everyone know we're on our way."

Justin was somewhat surprised. He had never known Jackie to think up such a daring plan before. But he reasoned if she thought they could do it, they could do it. "It's so we can let our parents know about the blackfly guy, right?" he said.

Jackie nodded, a trace of worry on her face. "I just hope we make it to the junction in time," she said.

"Then why is Grace already turning left now?" Justin said.

"Already?" Jackie said. "Yes! This is it!" She called out to Grace. "Meet you all at the campground!"

Without looking back, Grace lifted an arm and

gave Jackie a thumbs-up.

Jackie looked at Justin. “Are you ready?” she said.

“I think so,” Justin said. Dax was looking up at him from the pack basket. “Are you ready, girl?” She blinked.

As the last bike made the turn, Justin looked back and noticed some movement on the trail behind them. “I think I see him!” he said.

“Here we go!” Jackie said.

Nick was puzzled as his group came to a halt not far along on the Eagles Nest Lake trail. He glanced back just in time to see Jackie and Justin speed by. “Hey, where are they going?” he said.

“Nick, wait!” Grace said. But it was too late. He had already taken off after them.

## Chapter Nineteen

# Bye-Bye Blackfly Bad Guy

"What are you doing, Nick?" Justin said. At first he thought he heard the blackfly guy already gaining on them, and then realized who it was. He wished he'd felt relief when he discovered it was only their friend, but he wasn't relieved at all and blurted out, "You're ruining the plan."

Nick didn't care. "What plan?" he said, and grunted as he hit another rough spot in the pathway in his frantic attempt to catch up to them. "You're not leaving me behind."

"Forget it, Justin," Jackie said. "Nick can't go back now. We all just have to keep moving – fast."

The rocks and roots of the bumpy trail were never kind to any of the youth bicycles, or to the young riders. And especially not now that in their great haste each of their tires were striking so many of them. Pedals were being pummeled, chains strained and rims rattled with every revolution of every wheel.

"Why are we speeding?" Nick said. "I can't keep going like this."

"I'll tell you why," Justin said. "The blackfly guy is right behind us."

Nick's ears prickled. "He is?" he said. "We're doomed!" And suddenly he was rolling past Justin.

As the path finally flattened out and the ride became easier, it occurred to Justin the ride was probably a lot easier for the blackfly guy with his giant pack as well.

It was.

With Jackie and Nick now in front of him, Justin knew the metallic clicking sound pressing in on him from behind was not from any animal. It had to be a bicycle. He cried out to Jackie. "How much further!" he said.

Jackie noticed a slight break in the trees and knew they were approaching the Seventh Lake inlet. "We still have quite a ways to go to get to the campground," she said.

As the racing trio approached the trail's final wooden bridge, Justin noticed the straps holding the pack basket in place on the handlebars of his bike were coming loose – very loose. So loose, in fact, that the pack basket was beginning to tip sideways.

He quickly discovered keeping the bouncing bike steady with one hand while pedaling like mad and trying to keep the basket upright with the other hand was proving impossible.

Dax, who had shown hints she was not at all enjoying this latest leg of the **Bug Lake Bike Race**, was definitely transmitting those negative signals now.

As the front wheel wobbled, Justin could feel

the basket slipping from his grasp. He could tell Dax knew it, too, and the panicked cat lover recognized the position of his dear pet's body having seen it many times before. She was poised and getting ready to jump.

Bursting from the woods, Jackie was first to hit the three raised planks that ran down the center of the wooden bridge.

Nick emerged next and followed her across the inlet.

Then it was Justin's turn and he hit the planks at an awkward angle causing the bike to jerk sideways. He had to let go of the pack basket to regain control and that's when Dax did it. She jumped.

"Dax!" Justin cried as he skidded to a halt in the grass across the inlet, the pack basket dangling from the handlebars.

The athletic calico was fine having landed upright near the center of the bridge.

Upon hearing Justin's cry, Jackie and Nick had slammed on their brakes as well.

"Go get her," Jackie said to Justin, as she dropped her bike. "I'll fix the pack basket."

Justin began his dash onto the bridge to rescue Dax, when a fourth bike – a large bike – carrying a big guy – with a massive backpack – shot out of the woods and hit the wooden bridge with enough force that it actually made the entire structure shake.

Three stunned Adirondack kids watched as one very stunned rider yanked his handlebars sideways, swerving wildly to avoid the cat, and launched from the side of the bridge into the chilly water of the inlet.

As the man and his equipment separated in mid-air, there were three distinct and enormous splashes, and it seemed to Justin that the landings took forever.

First, it was the bike. *Ka-Splash.*

Next, it was the backpack. *Ka-Splash.*

And finally, it was the blackfly guy. *KA-SPASH!*

It took a moment for the drenched rider to orient himself and then he stood in the shallows, a dark cloud of blackflies surrounding his dripping head.

## Chapter Twenty

# Pack Open – Case Closed

Justin muttered a brief apology to the blackfly guy who was wading toward his sinking backpack. "Sorry," he said as he scooped up Dax in his arms and hurried back to his bike.

"Let's go," Nick said.

"Wait," Jackie said. "Listen."

*Ring-ring. Ring-ring.*

As the blackfly guy began collecting floating objects and stuffing them back into his waterlogged pack, Mattie, Grace, Addison and Aiden casually crossed the bridge, and in that order.

*Ring-ring. Ring-ring.* Mattie gave the wading blackfly guy a big smile and a wave.

It didn't take long for the whole group of riders to travel the final mild section of the trail to find smiling and familiar faces awaiting them at the campground finish line.

While approaching the small but enthusiastic crowd, Justin could feel his whole body relax as soon as he saw his parents.

Jackie was glad to see her parents there as well.

But she was almost more excited to notice in the gathering someone else who had decided to attend the event. "Ranger Buck is here!" she said.

Nick was quick to recognize the reporter from the local newspaper. "You did it, Jackie," he said. "You got Miss Carolyn to come." Then he saw her camera pointed their way. "We'd all better smile." He plastered on a big grin.

No one had to tell Mattie to smile. "I see Mom and Dad," she said, and started ringing her bell like crazy.

Coasting to a stop amidst the applause, Jackie motioned to her parents to join her as she parked her bike and made a dash for Ranger Buck.

Nick headed for the reporter.

Justin set Dax free from the pack basket and smiled as Grace escorted Mattie to her anxious parents.

He saw R.J. standing with two elderly people he assumed were his grandparents, and Aiden was pointing at his sister in an accusatory manner before another pair of adults.

Trotting to greet his own mom and dad, Justin noticed Ranger Buck had already hustled to his truck and was talking on his radio. Nick and the reporter were at his side.

Before Justin could explain anything to his parents, Jackie returned to the finish line and politely interrupted the assortment of reunions that were taking place. "Excuse me," she said. "If we can have everyone gather over at the picnic area, my mom said the food is all ready. Right after eating, we'll announce the winner of the **Bug Lake Bike Race**."

There was dead silence, and from the looks on everyone's faces, Jackie was concerned she had just said something terribly wrong. Then she realized no one was paying attention to her at all. There was a squeaking noise behind her and the buzzing of blackflies. She turned to see what everyone else was staring at.

It was the blackfly guy, still soaking wet and struggling to march his bike forward — a very difficult thing to do with a twisted front rim and a saturated pack on your back.

*Ring-ring. Ring-ring.* "That man was swimming," Mattie said.

Because he was wearing sunglasses, no one could tell who or what the young man with the personal halo of blackflies might be looking at, but everyone could see where he was headed. Without saying a word, he pushed through the crowd toward a brown van with a bicycle rack that was parked all alone by the restroom facilities.

"Follow the aroma now everybody." It was Jackie's mother now extending the invitation, and at first everyone looked at Nick. "To the picnic area," she quickly said.

As the people began to walk toward the cookout, Ranger Buck took purposeful steps toward the blackfly guy.

Justin and Jackie joined Nick and the reporter at a safe distance behind him.

The blackfly guy had already loaded his heavy pack into the back of the van and was beginning to close the door.

"Please leave that door open," Ranger Buck said. "I'd like to ask you a few questions."

The blackfly guy turned and smiled. "Yes?" he said.

Ranger Buck was not smiling. "Would you take those sunglasses off while I'm speaking with you?" he said.

The Adirondack kids could tell this was a serious moment.

As the blackfly guy removed his sunglasses, an Inlet police car pulled into the campground and parked near the van.

The crowd returned to see what was happening and the blackfly guy's smile suddenly disappeared.

"That's him, Miss Carolyn," Jackie said. "He's the one who nearly ran us over yesterday at the **Black Fly Challenge™**."

"Move back, folks," the officer said as he got out of the car and walked to assist the ranger.

"You're absolutely right, Jackie," Miss Carolyn said, and moved to get a better angle on the action.

"Did you see the banner?" Nick asked his friends.

"How could we?" Justin said. "You were the only one who saw it."

"No," Nick said. "Didn't you see it just now sticking out of the top of his backpack?"

"I think they're looking at it now," Jackie said.

Everyone watched as the ranger and officer had

the top of the backpack wide open and unfurled a large piece of white canvas exposing the familiar red and blue lettering.

"That's it," Justin said. "They got the banner."

The officer then entered the back of the van.

"What's he doing now?" Nick said.

"Let's find out," Jackie said, and the trio moved to be near Miss Carolyn who had a direct view of the back of the van and was snapping picture after picture. The officer was busy uncovering a large object that appeared to be wrapped in several layers of sheets and blankets.

"That guy has a mummy in there," Nick said.

As the final sheet was being peeled away, Justin's eyes grew wide. "I think it's Bug-Eye," he said.

More of the creature's unique shape and colors were being uncovered and revealed, and Nick began giving a piece-by-piece report. "Black body," he said. "Greenish wing... Red Seat... Gigantic blue eyes!"

"It *is* Bug-Eye," Jackie said.

"Do you mean the animal carving that was taken from the Adirondack Carousel?" Miss Carolyn said.

"Yes!" Justin said.

"Now I remember that guy," Nick said. "He was the one at the carousel who was so mad at Justin for always beating him to ride Bug-Eye!"

"Well, Jackie," Miss Carolyn said, "I am so very grateful you invited me to your event today." As she talked, she continued to snap pictures of the bandit and the rescued blackfly. "You've provided me with two big stories in the same place and on the same day. How does this sound for a news article headline?" She lowered her camera and turned to the Adirondack kids. "*'The Carousel Case, The Bicycle Race and the Blackfly Bad Guy.'*"

"Pretty good," Nick said.

"I like it," Jackie said.

Justin agreed. "I like it a lot," he said. "It sounds like it could even be a book."

## Chapter Twenty-One

# Full Circle

"This is indeed a happy day for all of us here at the Adirondack Carousel," said Paula Hameline, executive director for the tourist attraction and educational center. "And we are so pleased so many of you could join us this afternoon to celebrate the return of Bug-Eye to his home in Saranac Lake." She turned and motioned toward the blackfly behind her that had been remounted on the deck of the ride.

There was applause from the nearly one hundred people who were gathered at dining tables that were set up in a large semi-circle all around the carousel.

Reporters from several local newspapers were also present, including Miss Carolyn from the *Weekly Adirondack.*

"Now I'd like to introduce to you Miss Jackie Salsberry from Inlet," the director said. "Jackie and her friends were largely responsible for making this day possible, and she has a statement and a few announcements to make."

There was more applause as Jackie stood up from

where she was seated with Justin and Nick and walked toward the podium.

Justin was amazed at Jackie's poise as she stood in front of the crowd. Of course, he had always been amazed at her and was so proud she was one of his very best friends.

"Thank you for having us here today, Mrs. Hameline," Jackie began. She had notes on small cards in front of her, but did not appear to need them. "My friends and I are really grateful for your generosity, inviting us to this big party and letting us ride the carousel all day." She looked out over the crowd. "Could all of you who were in the Bug Lake race, please stand?"

They all were there: Justin, Jackie, Nick, Mattie, Aiden, Addison and Grace, along with members from their families. Even R.J. was there, who was able to make the short trip with his grandparents from Vermont.

Nick shouted through the applause. "Go, Jackie!" he said, and then whispered to Justin. "What does *generosity* mean?"

"Shhh," Justin said.

They all sat down and Jackie continued. "Two weeks ago we had our **Bug Lake Bike Race** with an animal scavenger hunt near where I live in Inlet," she said. "And because of all of the things that happened at the end of the race, which most of you already know about, we never finished our picnic or announced the race winner."

Justin overheard an older adult whispering at a table next to him. "Can you believe that for years that thief has travelled and taken blackfly artifacts from festivals and events in six different states?" the lady said. "And then just to store them all in a cabin in the middle of the Wisconsin woods! What a strange thing to do."

Nick poked Justin in the arm and regained his attention. "I hope I won the race," he said. "I heard there is going to be a big surprise."

Justin began to take a drink of red punch from his cup. Glancing over, he noticed not only Nick's fingers were crossed, but so were his arms and legs. He tried not to laugh, but when Nick looked over at him with his eyes crossed as well, he couldn't help it. Justin managed to stifle the sound of his laugh, but not without some red punch forcing its way through his nose.

Jackie saw it all happen, but maintained her composure. "My hope for our race was that rather than just rush through the woods, we would take our time and discover some of the great and wonderful things that would be along the trail all around us," she said. "And we did. There were lots of great photos taken by the riders for the scavenger hunt – everything from an eagle to a white-tailed deer."

"An eagle?" Nick said. "Who got a picture of Soarin?" He saw the puzzled look on Justin's face and pointed to the bird on the carousel that was positioned behind Bug-Eye. "Soarin is the name of the eagle."

Justin shook his head. "What have you done?" he said. "Memorized the name of all the creatures on the ride?"

"Almost," Nick said, and grinned.

"In fact," Jackie said, and turned to look at the carousel, "there were pictures taken of almost every Adirondack animal here. At least all of the smaller animals."

Nick moaned. "There's no way I'm going to win," he said.

Jackie moved on to close her short speech. "Our original plan was to give every racer a point for each animal seen and photographed," she said. "The one with the most points would be named the race winner." She motioned to Mrs. Hameline to join her back at the podium. "But thanks to the board members here at the carousel and a few local bookstores, I am glad to announce that everyone who was in the **Bug Lake Bike Race** is going to be a winner."

Nick was stunned. "We are?" he said.

"That's right," Mrs. Hameline said. "Each one who participated in the Bug Lake race in Inlet will receive a sweatshirt and a hat, compliments of the carousel, along with tickets to ride any day we are open the rest of the year."

"And from the bookstores," Jackie added, "everyone who was in the race will also get a field guide to the animals of the Adirondacks."

There was cheering and applause from every table.

"Once again, Jackie and friends," Mrs. Hameline

said, "our sincere thanks for the safe return of Bug-Eye." Music began to take over the sound system and the carousel slowly began to turn. "Now, let's get this party started!"

# Epilogue

As most of the kids rushed to get on the carousel, Justin decided to wait and see what animals everyone else would pick to ride. This time, he would take whatever creature might be left.

He wasn't surprised to see Nick head straight for Lucy.

Addison was pushing her brother, Aiden, to get on Paws, the black bear. He thought the perfect animal for her to get on would be Spike, the prickly porcupine. And after settling her teary-eyed brother into the seat of the bear, she did.

He noticed Mattie was having a hard time trying to decide which animal to ride. "I love lady bugs," he heard her say. Then he realized why she was having such a difficult time choosing an animal to ride. It looked like *every* creature had a lady bug placed somewhere in its design. She finally settled on Shelly, the turtle, when she discovered there were two ladybugs carved right below its saddle.

After the unkind thing R.J. had said to him on the trail about Nick and his foul odor, Justin thought it was kind of funny he was sitting on Spencer – the skunk!

Grace had selected Ranger, the raccoon, and Justin was pretty sure it was because Jackie was sitting in front of her on Twitter, the Hermit Thrush.

Jackie made eye contact with him and gestured to the lonely creature sitting next to her and with a look that said, "Aren't you coming aboard?"

Justin couldn't believe it. He'd given everyone else a chance at it first.

"Hurry up, Justin," Jackie said.

Justin didn't need any more encouragement and made a beeline for the only animal on the carousel that was left untaken – Bug-Eye, the blackfly.

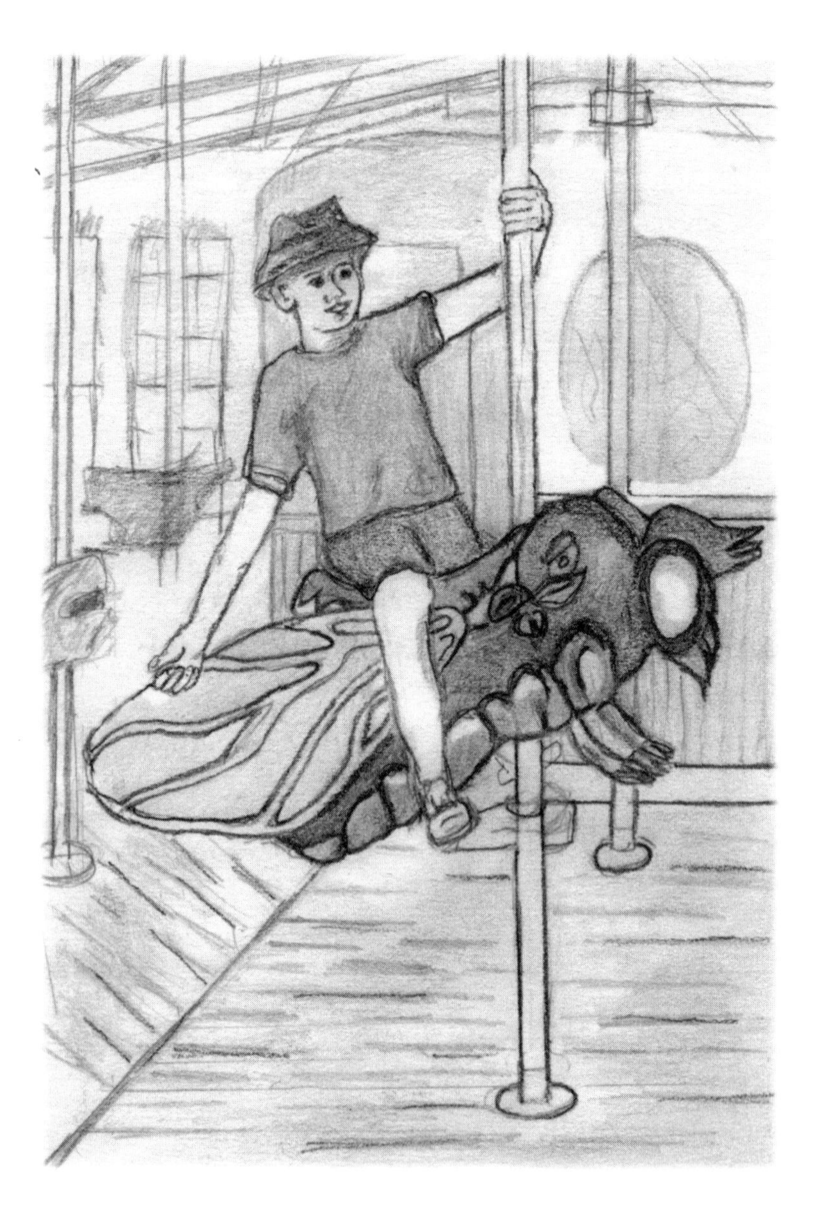

Justin and Bug-Eye

## The Black Fly Challenge™

**The Black Fly Challenge™** is a 40-mile mountain bike race that has been held in the middle of black-fly season since it began in 1996. It is on the second Saturday each June when hundreds of participants on all kinds of bikes ride the challenging route through the Moose River Plains between the communities of Inlet and Indian Lake, New York. Each year the race reverses direction. For more information on The Black Fly Challenge™ visit:

www.blackflychallenge.com
or the Inlet Information Center
at www.inletny.com

The starting line of the annual Black Fly Challenge™ 40-mile race. *Photo © 2013 Gary VanRiper*

# The Adirondack Carousel

The **Adirondack Carousel** in Saranac Lake, New York officially opened to the public in May of 2012. Throughout the year the young and the young at heart can ride any one of eighteen of the twenty-four different handcrafted Adirondack animals that were fashioned by woodcarvers for the full-size carousel. There is also a wheelchair accessible chariot on board playfully named, *See-Ya-Round*.

The first creature to be completed for the Adirondack Carousel was Bug-Eye, the blackfly!

*Photo © 2013 Gary VanRiper*

The Adirondack Carousel in Saranac Lake. *Photo © 2013 Gary VanRiper*

More than a tourist attraction, the large pavilion housing the carousel is also used for special programs and events which fulfill the mission and vision of its founders:

> *To fuse art, education and entertainment, and involve, encourage and inspire all youth to appreciate where we live, to be environmentally responsible, to enjoy the great outdoors, and to have fun while doing it.*

The Adirondack Carousel is located at 2 Depot Street, Saranac Lake, NY 12983. For more information, visit www.adirondackcarousel.org

## Eastern Tiger Swallowtail Butterfly

The **Eastern Tiger Swallowtail Butterfly** is one of the easiest butterflies to identify. The males are bright yellow with four black tiger stripes, and during an Adirondack spring, they may be seen in great numbers. They can also draw attention because they like to rest with those bright yellow wings wide open. Female Eastern Tiger Swallowtails are not as easy to find, since they are very dark in color. Like the common Monarch butterfly, the Tiger Swallowtail can be found throughout most of North America.

**Eastern Tiger Swallowtail.** *Photo © 2013 Gary VanRiper*

These Eastern Tiger Swallowtails are puddling! You may find a puddle club on wet soil where the male butterflies are gathering to obtain much needed salts and minerals.
*Photo used by permission © 2013 Gary Lee*

## About the Cover Illustrator

**Susan Loeffler** is a freelance illustrator who lives in Central New York. Her full-color cover illustrations appear on every book in *The Adirondack Kids*® series, including the cover of *The Adirondack Kids*® coloring book, Runaway Dax, which also features her interior black-and-white illustrations.

# About the Authors

**Gary and Justin VanRiper** are a father-and-son writing team residing with their family and cat, Dax, in Camden, New York. They spend many summer and autumn days at camp on Fourth Lake in the Adirondacks.

**The Adirondack Kids® writing and illustrating team. From left: Gary, Carol and Justin VanRiper.**

*Photograph © Adirondack Kids Press, Ltd.*

*The Adirondack Kids®* began as a writing exercise at home when Justin was in third grade. Encouraged after a public reading of the piece at a Parents As Reading Partners (PARP) event at school, the project grew into a middle-reader chapter book series.

The fifth book in the series, *Islands in the Sky*, won the 2005–06 Adirondack Literary Award for Best Children's Book. Books in the series are used in schools throughout the state of New York and titles also regularly appear on the New York State Charlotte Award's Suggested Reading List. More than 115,000 of *The Adirondack Kids®* books have been sold.

The authors often visit elementary schools, libraries and conferences to encourage students to read and inspire them to write.

The Adirondack Kids

The Adirondack Kids #4
The Great Train Robbery
JUSTIN AND GARY VANRIPER • Illustrated by Carol VanRiper

The Adirondack Kids #5
Islands in the Sky

The Adirondack Kids #6
Secret of the Skeleton Key